# The
# Tiara
# Club
### ✦ AT SILVER TOWERS ✦

## The Tiara Club

Princess Charlotte *and the* Birthday Ball

Princess Katie *and the* Silver Pony

Princess Daisy *and the* Dazzling Dragon

Princess Sophia *and the* Sparkling Surprise

Princess Alice *and the* Magical Mirror

Princess Emily *and the* Substitute Fairy

## The Tiara Club at Silver Towers

Princess Charlotte *and the* Enchanted Rose

Princess Katie *and the* Mixed-up Potion

Princess Daisy *and the* Magical Merry-Go-Round

Princess Sophia *and the* Prince's Party

Princess Emily *and the* Wishing Star

~ VIVIAN FRENCH ~

# The
# *Tiara*
# *Club*

✦ AT SILVER TOWERS ✦

*Princess Alice*
~ AND THE ~
*Glass Slipper*

ILLUSTRATED BY SARAH GIBB

KATHERINE TEGEN BOOKS
■ HarperTrophy®
*An Imprint of* HarperCollins*Publishers*

The Tiara Club at Silver Towers:
Princess Alice and the Glass Slipper
Text copyright © 2007 by Vivian French
Illustrations copyright © 2007 by Sarah Gibb

Library of Congress Cataloging-in-Publication Data
French, Vivian.
    Princess Alice and the glass slipper / by Vivian French ; illus-
trated by Sarah Gibb. — 1st U.S. ed.
        p. cm. — (Tiara Club at Silver Towers)
    "Katherine Tegen books."
    Summary: During a field trip to the Museum of Royal Life,
Princess Alice is blamed for breaking the case that holds
Cinderella's glass slipper.
    ISBN 978-0-06-112447-1
    [1. Princesses—Fiction. 2. School field trips—Fiction.]
I. Gibb, Sarah, ill. II. Title.
PZ7.F88917Prah 2007                          2007011862
[Fic]—dc22                                           CIP
                                                            AC

Typography by Amy Ryan
❖
First U.S. edition, 2007

*For my very own Princess Alice,*
*with all my love, Mom xx*
*—V.F.*

*For Janet*
*and little Prince Leandro, x*
*—S.G.*

# The Royal Palace Academy
## *for the* Preparation of Perfect Princesses
### (Known to our students as "The Princess Academy")

## OUR SCHOOL MOTTO:
*A Perfect Princess always thinks of others before herself,
and is kind, caring, and truthful.*

Silver Towers offers a complete education for
Tiara Club princesses with emphasis on
selected outings. The curriculum includes:

*Fans and Curtseys*

*A visit to Witch Windlespin*
*(Royal herbalist, healer, and maker of magic potions)*

*Problem Prime Ministers*

*A visit to the Museum of Royal Life*
*(Students will be well protected from the Poisoned Apple)*

Our principal, Queen Samantha Joy, is present
at all times, and students are in the excellent care
of the school Fairy Godmother, Fairy Angora.

### OUR RESIDENT STAFF & VISITING EXPERTS INCLUDE:

LADY ALBINA MacSPLINTER *(School Secretary)*

CROWN PRINCE DANDINO *(Field Trips)*

QUEEN MOTHER MATILDA *(Etiquette, Posture, and Poise)*

FAIRY G. *(Head Fairy Godmother)*

We award tiara points to encourage our
Tiara Club princesses toward the next level.
All princesses who win enough points at Silver
Towers will attend the Silver Ball, where they
will be presented with their Silver Sashes.

Silver Sash Tiara Club princesses are invited
to return to Ruby Mansions, our exclusive
residence for Perfect Princesses, where they may
continue their education at a higher level.

PLEASE NOTE:

Princesses are expected to arrive
at the Academy with a *minimum* of:

TWENTY BALL GOWNS
*(with all necessary hoops,
petticoats, etc.)*

TWELVE DAY-DRESSES

SEVEN GOWNS
*suitable for garden parties
and other special daytime
occasions*

TWELVE TIARAS

DANCING SHOES
*five pairs*

VELVET SLIPPERS
*three pairs*

RIDING BOOTS
*two pairs*

*Cloaks, muffs, stoles, gloves,
and other essential
accessories, as required*

Hi! How are you doing? It's great that you're here at Silver Towers—you're a real STAR. Not like the twins, Princess Diamonde and Princess Gruella. They're so stuck up and mean. Sometimes I almost hope they won't get enough tiara points to get their Silver Sashes and go on to Ruby Mansions, but that's not the way a Perfect Princess ought to think!

Oh, I forgot to say. I'm Princess Alice and I share the Silver Rose Room with Charlotte, Katie, Daisy, Sophia, and Emily. They're my best friends, and we try to do everything together.

## Chapter One

𝒟o you go on field trips? Ever since we've been at Silver Towers, we've had one trip after another. Our principal, Queen Samantha Joy, says that it's good for us, and they usually end up being really fun! But we were seriously excited when Queen Samantha Joy told us we were going to go to King Rudolfo the Third's private Museum of Royal Life. My big sister went there when she was at Silver Towers (she's at Ruby Mansions now), and she said it was amazing! She saw the Poisoned Apple, the Glass Slipper, the Spinning Wheel, and lots of other really fantastic things.

Lady Albina (she's Queen Samantha Joy's secretary and she organizes us with about fifty thousand lists every single day) heard me telling my friends about the museum after morning assembly was over, and she frowned at me.

She's always frowning, unless she's talking to Queen Samantha Joy.

"Princess Alice, I hope you don't think you know everything already!" she snapped.

I heard Princess Diamonde snicker and whisper, "She doesn't, but *we* do, don't we?" to Princess Gruella, but I pretended I hadn't heard.

"Oh, no! I really don't," I said, and curtsied to Lady Albina.

"I'm glad to hear it! That is how mistakes are made! Tomorrow you will be divided into groups. Each group will have a questionnaire to complete, and tiara points will be awarded for the best answers. And"—Lady Albina looked even more disapproving—"King Rudolfo has offered a prize. A quite unnecessary prize, if you ask me."

"A prize?" We clustered around Lady Albina. Even Diamonde and Gruella looked excited. "Please, Lady Albina, what is it?"

Lady Albina sniffed. "The winning group will be invited to take part in King Rudolfo's Annual Royal Parade. They will ride in the Golden Pumpkin Coach."

A royal parade! And a golden pumpkin coach! It sounded so wonderful. We couldn't help talking about it every time we had a spare moment in between classes, and that night we were too excited to sleep.

"We will be in the same group, right?" Princess Daisy asked. "It would be awful if we weren't."

"Of course we will be," Princess

Emily said reassuringly. "Lady Albina chooses by dormitories."

"Hurrah for the Silver Rose Roomers!" Princess Katie cheered. "And you know all about the museum, Alice, so we'll have a really good chance of winning."

I shook my head. "I only know what my big sister said."

"Is everything in glass cases?" Princess Charlotte asked. "Or can we touch the things?"

"No!" Princess Sophia looked horrified. "Imagine touching a poisoned apple!"

Emily giggled. "We'd all fall over and look as if we were dead, and have to wait to be kissed by a handsome—"

She was interrupted by a knock on the door, and Fairy Angora appeared. She's our school Fairy Godmother and she keeps an eye on us all.

"Too much noise, my precious darlings," she said. "It's time to go to sleep."

She waved her wand and a drift of twinkly sparkles floated into the air and I suddenly couldn't keep my eyes open a second longer.

# Chapter Two

*I* had the weirdest dream! I was wearing a pair of absolutely gorgeous glass slippers and I was dancing all by myself in the middle of a huge ballroom and then I felt someone shaking me.

"Alice! Wake up. Come on!" It was Charlotte. "The bell's rung—you've got to get up! It's the visit to the museum today—we've got to hurry!"

I forgot all about my dream and rushed out of bed.

Lady Albina fussed about, giving out questionnaires and pencils and instructions the whole time we were eating our breakfast. Honestly, it almost made me not want to go. Luckily, Crown Prince Dandino

came bouncing into the breakfast hall just as we finished. He organizes our school trips—and he's really fun.

"Everyone ready for a fabulous day out?" he asked. "We're going to King Rudolfo's library first, to see some of his books. Then we'll visit the museum, and you can have a good look at the exhibits. At the end of the morning, we'll meet up back in the library. You can finish filling out your questionnaires while you're there. Lunch will be in the state dining room, and afterward you can wander around the gardens while King Rudolfo and I look at your work. We'll announce the tiara

points awarded and the winners of
the competition at a little ceremony
before we all go home!"

I was really glad when we finally
rolled up the enormous driveway
to King Rudolfo's palace. All of us
Silver Rose Roomers were in the
same coach, and so were Princess

Jemima, Princess Lisa, Princess Freya, and Princess Chloe. Unfortunately, the twins were there as well, and Diamonde spent the whole journey telling us how she and Gruella had been to the museum before.

"Of course," Diamonde boasted, "we had tea with King Rudy, didn't we, Gruella?"

Gruella nodded enthusiastically. "King Rudy gave us fifteen different kinds of cake."

"I thought he was called King Rudolfo," Emily said.

"He is, but his special friends call him King Rudy, and Mommy's one

of his most special friends."
Diamonde looked so pleased with
herself as she sat back, looking as
if she was expecting a round of
applause.

"That's nice," Daisy said, but
she didn't sound very impressed.

Diamonde leaned forward and went on boasting.

"*And* he let us hold the pea that was under the mattresses, and look in the magic mirror, and do whatever we wanted. Didn't he, Gruella?"

Gruella nodded again, but it was odd. She was suddenly looking a bit uncomfortable.

Diamonde coughed loudly. "Ahem! And do you know what else? King Rudy even let me try on the Glass Slipper!"

"Amazing!" said Princess Chloe, her eyes very big and round. "Did he really?"

Diamonde smiled a smug smile. "It fit me *perfectly*."

I hadn't been paying her much attention because I was wondering what was wrong with Gruella, but that made me sit up.

"You couldn't have worn the

slipper," I said, surprised. "I really want to try it, but my big sister told me nobody's ever allowed to."

Diamonde turned bright red and glared at me. "Well, I did! Didn't I, Gruella?" And I was sure I saw her pinch her twin.

"Oh . . . yes," Gruella said, nodding.

"You'll see!" Diamonde hissed at me. "Just because you've got a big sister doesn't mean you know everything."

I didn't answer. I was almost certain Diamonde had been telling lies, and when I looked at my friends' faces I knew they thought so too.

# Chapter Three

*A*s soon as the coach stopped, Diamonde grabbed Gruella, and the two of them pushed their way out before the rest of us had even picked up our bags.

An incredibly tall, thin king wearing horn-rimmed glasses was leaning against the wall. Diamonde practically elbowed Prince Dandino out of the way as she dashed toward the king.

"King Rudy!" she squealed, and sank into a curtsey. "Mommy says she's just dying to see you again!"

A nasty little part of me was

hoping King Rudolfo would say, "Who? What? Who are you?" but he didn't. He smiled a rather absent-minded smile and said, "Many thanks, my dear, many thanks indeed." He took off his glasses, cleaned them, and put them back on and peered at the rest of us.

"Welcome to you all," he said. "We'll start in the library, shall we?"

Number one on our questionnaire was, "How many books are there in King Rudolfo's library?" and I was very glad we didn't have to count them, because there were thousands. He told us there were about fifty thousand, but he couldn't be certain.

"Excuse me, Your Majesty," I said, "but might I ask how many you've read?"

Diamonde gave a little shriek. "Oh, Alice! You can't mean your super-special big sister didn't tell you? King Rudy's got much more important things to do than read books, haven't you, King Rudy?"

King Rudolfo looked at Diamonde in a puzzled sort of way.

"Actually, my dear," he said, "I think reading is a delightful thing to do. There isn't much you can't learn from a book. Now, shall I let you all wander around? My house-keeper will bring you something to drink soon." And he patted Diamonde on the head as he walked away.

Diamonde looked annoyed for a moment, then waved her arm at the books as if they belonged to her.

"Shall I show you around?" she

said. "After all, Gruella and I have
been here before."

"No, thank you," I said. "We'll

look for ourselves." And I was sorry if that sounded rude, but I was getting fed up with Diamonde being such a show-off.

"Ooooooh." Diamonde sneered. "Guess who thinks her big sister has told her everything there is to know!"

I didn't answer. I took Charlotte's arm and we went to look at a row of pictures of King Rudolfo's family. Daisy, Emily, Katie, and Sophia came with us, and we studied the huge paintings carefully.

"Look!" Daisy said. "All of King

Rudolfo's relatives are holding books."

Katie chuckled. "So that's question number two answered. 'How do King Rudolfo's family members entertain themselves when they are relaxing?'"

"I wish we could go to the museum," I said. "I'm dying to see the Glass Slipper!"

And just as if she'd heard me, at that moment the housekeeper came in with a tray of juice and cookies.

"I've just opened the museum," she announced as she put the tray down. "King Rudolfo says he'll be back in twenty minutes or so to show you around."

"Do we have to wait for him?" I asked.

The housekeeper smiled at me.

"You can wait for him in the museum if you've finished up here. It's just down the corridor and through the swinging doors."

We looked at one another.

"Do you want a snack?" I asked. "Or shall we go now?"

"Let's go now!" Emily said, and Sophia, Daisy, Katie, and Charlotte nodded.

# Chapter Four

The museum wasn't very big, but it was absolutely crammed with glass cases, and the walls had shelves reaching right up to the ceiling. It was quite scary; the shelves were piled so high with papers and boxes and bits and pieces I couldn't help thinking we'd be completely buried if they fell down. It felt more like a workroom or a study than a museum, and we found ourselves whispering as we tiptoed around.

"Wow!" Charlotte was staring into a little silver container. "Here's a pea! It says it's the actual pea the princess felt under all the mattresses."

Sophia came to look. "It's all shriveled," she said doubtfully.

Katie pointed to a corner. "That's the Spinning Wheel!"

We went to look, and she was right. Next to it was a tower of pure

gold plates, all with the most com-
plicated royal crests.

"It says these came from
Cinderella's wedding," Daisy whispered as she read the label.

Sleeping Beauty

Cinderella's Wedding Plates

"There's half an apple on that shelf," Katie whispered back. "Do you—"

She stopped because Diamonde and Gruella were standing in the doorway and there was something

very sneaky about the way they were looking around.

We didn't mean to spy on them. We really, really didn't, although I suppose if we'd been truly Perfect Princesses we'd have stepped forward and said hello as soon as we saw them. Instead, we stayed in our dark corner and watched to see what they were up to.

"King Rudy won't be here for at least ten minutes," Diamonde said. "We've got lots of time." And she put up her hand and turned on the light.

It made such a difference! There was a beautiful chandelier in the middle of the room, and it glittered and shone and sent sparkles of light flashing over the glass cases. It lit up a tall case that was immediately beneath it, and I don't know why Diamonde and Gruella didn't hear us as we *oooh*ed and *aaah*ed. The

Glass Slipper was so beautiful, I don't know how we could possibly have missed it when we first came in.

I was just moving out of our dark corner when Katie pulled me back.

"Look at Diamonde!" she hissed

in my ear. I looked, and my mouth dropped wide open.

Diamonde was trying to lift up the glass cover over the Glass Slipper!

"Come here!" she snapped at Gruella. "Can't you see I need help?"

Gruella didn't look at all happy. "I don't think—" she began, but Diamonde didn't notice.

"I told Chloe I'd already worn the Glass Slipper," she said, "and I'm going to wear it, so there."

She gave the glass cover one last heave, lifted it off, and dropped it!

Shards of glass flew everywhere,

and the crash was tremendous. Daisy screamed and Emily shrieked, and Charlotte, Sophia, Katie, and I gasped as we hurried over. At once, Diamonde snatched up the slipper and pushed it into my hands. When Prince Dandino

and King Rudolfo came hurrying
in a second later, followed by all
the Silver Towers Princesses, there
I was, standing in the middle of
a pile of shattered glass, clutching
the Glass Slipper.

As everyone stared and stared

and stared at me, Diamonde said, "She told us she'd always wanted to try on the slipper. We all heard her, didn't we, Chloe?"

What could poor Chloe say? She turned bright red and nodded. Prince Dandino folded his arms and frowned at me.

"I can't say how disappointed I am, Princess Alice. I've always thought of you as one of our star pupils, but this is a terrible, terrible thing to have done!"

I didn't know what to do. I couldn't say it was Diamonde who had broken the glass case, because that would have been tattling, and I knew my friends would feel exactly the same way. I stared down at the Glass Slipper and I was so confused and angry and embarrassed, I began to blush.

"See?" Diamonde sounded triumphant. "She's turned all red!"

"Princess Alice, I think you'd

better go straight to the library," Prince Dandino said sternly. "And when we get back to Silver Towers, we'll see what Queen Samantha Joy has to say."

"Yes, Your Highness," I said. I was about to curtsey when I remembered I was still holding the Glass Slipper. I held it out to King Rudolfo.

"Please excuse me, Your Majesty," I said. "And I am very, very sorry that this has happened."

King Rudolfo took the slipper and then he did such an odd thing. He gave me a little bow and said, "Before you retire to the library,

Princess Alice, would you like to try on the Glass Slipper?"

I couldn't believe my ears. I was so un-princessy! I really and truly gaped at him. Prince Dandino made a *tut-tut*ting noise. "I don't think Princess Alice deserves such

an honor, Your Majesty," he said.

King Rudolfo gave a funny little smile and said, "Please allow this, Prince Dandino. I have my reasons. This is a magic slipper."

So I took off my shoe, and King Rudolfo put the slipper onto my foot!

It was weird. It fit very well, but it was a little bit tight around my heel, and it felt so cold and hard.

I couldn't imagine how anybody could have danced in a pair of glass slippers. It only goes to show how very special the real owner must have been.

"Thank you," King Rudolfo said

as he gently took the slipper off again. "And now, would anyone else like to try?"

Of course, just about everyone put their hands up. King Rudolfo

beckoned to Diamonde.

"Why don't you try, Princess . . . oh, I'm so sorry." He shook his head. "I've forgotten your name."

Diamonde pouted, then smiled a forgiving smile. "I'm Queen Euphemia's daughter," she reminded him. "I'm Princess Diamonde. And I'd love to try on the Glass Slipper!"

# Chapter Five

And that was when I had the best idea. I wasn't going to tell on Diamonde, but I *was* going to make sure she didn't get away with everything.

I swept King Rudolfo my very best curtsey and I said, "Thank you for your kindness, King Rudolfo. It was most generous of you, and I have no right to ask anything of you, but as Princess Diamonde has already tried on the Glass Slipper before, might another princess have the honor, perhaps?"

King Rudolfo raised his eyebrows. "Princess Diamonde has already tried on the Glass Slipper?"

If looks could kill, I'd have been flat on the floor. Diamonde glared at me as she said, "But I haven't, Your Majesty. Princess Alice must be mistaken."

"No she isn't!" It was little Princess Chloe. "You told us you

did, Diamonde! When we were in the coach, remember? You said 'King Rudy' had let you try on the slipper and it fit you perfectly!"

There was a long pause. It was so

obvious that Diamonde had been telling lies. She turned absolutely red, and shuffled her feet, and muttered about only pretending. She said she hadn't really meant it.

King Rudolfo stroked his chin thoughtfully as he listened. Then he held the slipper out.

"Please put it on," he commanded.

Diamonde gulped. She took the slipper, put it on, and immediately began to hop and skip all over the broken glass.

"Help!" she squealed. "Help! I can't stop!" But it was no good.

Around and around the glass cases she danced, spinning in circles.

"Princess Diamonde! Stop this minute!" Prince Dandino roared. But it was no use. Poor Diamonde couldn't stop. King Rudolfo was frowning, but most of the Silver Towers Princesses were laughing and laughing and laughing. She did look funny, but it was horrible too because she looked so unhappy.

I ran to her and took her hand.

"I'll help you," I said. "Hold on to me and try to kick the slipper off!"

But Diamonde couldn't. The next thing I knew, I was hopping

and skipping as well, and when
Charlotte grabbed me she began
dancing too.

King Rudolfo held up his hand.
"I think," he said, "Princess

Diamonde has something to say."

And Diamonde, puffing hard, her face bright red and her hair a mess, said, "It was me! I broke the glass case! I'm very, very sorry."

She stopped at once and flopped

against me. Charlotte and I almost had to hold her up.

Prince Dandino strode across the room looking really angry, but I moved in front of Diamonde.

I couldn't help it.

I knew she was a show-off and told boastful lies, but I also knew how awful it must have been to have everyone laughing and not being able to stop.

"Please," I said. "Please don't be too mad at her. She didn't mean to break the glass, really she didn't."

King Rudolfo nodded.

"Princess Alice is quite right," he said. "Princess Diamonde has had punishment enough." He took my hand and kissed it.

"It's a delight to meet such a Perfect Princess."

"Me?" I said, surprised.

"A true princess never laughs at

the misfortunes of others, however well deserved those misfortunes may be." For a second, I thought I saw a tiny twinkle in his eye, but I might have been wrong. Then he continued.

"I suggest that Princess Alice's kindness be rewarded. Shall we forget the questionnaire, Prince Dandino, and ask Princess Alice and her friends to lead my Annual Royal Parade tomorrow and ride in the Golden Pumpkin Coach?"

## Chapter Six

So that was how Charlotte, Katie, Daisy, Sophia, Emily, and I spent the next day, and it was amazing! We spent the whole morning getting ready (we were wearing our very best dresses, and then at exactly twelve o'clock the Golden Pumpkin

Coach came rolling up to Silver
Towers, pulled by six beautiful
golden ponies. We settled ourselves

inside and then off we went all the
way through town, with the rest of
the Royal Parade marching and

dancing and singing behind us. There were thousands of people watching, and we bowed and smiled until our faces were sore. And at the end of the day, we went back to King Rudolfo's palace—

and guess what?!

Yes, we had the most amazing tea, and there were *thirty* different kinds of cake. Charlotte and I counted them.

And when we were finally driven back to Silver Towers, the house-keeper gave us the leftover cakes to share with all our other friends.

When it was bedtime, I found
Diamonde waiting for me by the
Silver Rose Room door. She looked

really awkward and embarrassed.

"I'm sorry," she mumbled, and
then she ran down the stairs as fast

as she could go.

And as I snuggled down in my bed, I thought how wonderful life was at Silver Towers, and I'm so glad you're here with us.

# What happens next?

### FIND OUT IN

## ✦ Princess Sophia ✦
#### ∾ AND THE ∾
## Prince's Party ✦

Hello! I'm Princess Sophia, and I'm
a Tiara Club princess here at
Silver Towers, just like you!
And I'm so glad you're here
with us.

I think you know my friends who share the
Silver Rose Room with me. There's Alice, and
Daisy, and Katie and Charlotte and Emily, and
I just know that if we get enough tiara points
to win our Silver Sashes and go on to Ruby
Mansions, we'll still be the very best friends
ever.

We're not too friendly with Princess
Diamonde and her twin sister, Gruella,
though. They just love showing off and being
mean.

# You are cordially invited
## to the Royal Princess Academy

**Follow the adventures of your special princess friends
as they try to earn enough points to join the Tiara Club.**

**Katherine Tegen Books**
*An Imprint of HarperCollinsPublishers*